Put Beginning Readers on the Right Track with ALL ABOARD READING™

The All Aboard Reading series is especially designed for beginning readers. Written by noted authors and illustrated in full color, these are books that children really want to read—books to excite their imagination, expand their interests, make them laugh, and support their feelings. With fiction and nonfiction stories that are high interest and curriculum-related, All Aboard Reading books offer something for every young reader. And with four different reading levels, the All Aboard Reading series lets you choose which books are most appropriate for your children and their growing abilities.

Picture Readers
Picture Readers have super-simple texts, with many nouns appearing as rebus pictures. At the end of each book are 24 flash cards—on one side is a rebus picture; on the other side is the written-out word.

Station Stop 1
Station Stop 1 books are best for children who have just begun to read. Simple words and big type make these early reading experiences more comfortable. Picture clues help children to figure out the words on the page. Lots of repetition throughout the text helps children to predict the next word or phrase—an essential step in developing word recognition.

Station Stop 2
Station Stop 2 books are written specifically for children who are reading with help. Short sentences make it easier for early readers to understand what they are reading. Simple plots and simple dialogue help children with reading comprehension.

Station Stop 3
Station Stop 3 books are perfect for children who are reading alone. With longer text and harder words, these books appeal to children who have mastered basic reading skills. More complex stories captivate children who are ready for more challenging books.

In addition to All Aboard Reading books, look for All Aboard Math Readers™ (fiction stories that teach math concepts children are learning in school); All Aboard Science Readers™ (nonfiction books that explore the most fascinating science topics in age-appropriate language); and All Aboard Poetry Readers™ (funny, rhyming poems for readers of all levels).

All Aboard for happy reading!

© 2004 The Wiggles Pty Ltd. U.S. Representative HIT Entertainment. All rights reserved. Published by Grosset & Dunlap, a division of Penguin Young Readers Group, 345 Hudson Street, New York, New York 10014. ALL ABOARD READING and GROSSET & DUNLAP are trademarks of Penguin Group (USA) Inc. Printed in the U.S.A.

Library of Congress Cataloging-in-Publication Data

Henry goes overboard / illustrated by Paul Nunn.
    p. cm. — (The Wiggles)
Summary: Henry the Octopus is tired of his job as conductor of the Underwater Big Band, and he and his Wiggles pals try to find a new job for him.
  ISBN 0-448-43525-X (pbk.)
  [1. Octopuses—Fiction. 2. Bands (Music)—Fiction. 3. Occupations—Fiction.] I. Nunn, Paul (Paul E.) ill. II. Series.
  PZ7.H39743 2004
  [E]—dc22
                                    2003021263

ISBN 0-448-43525-X   10 9 8 7 6 5 4 3 2 1

ALL ABOARD READING™

Station Stop
1

Illustrated by Paul E. Nunn

Grosset & Dunlap • New York

Henry the Octopus found a
book at the Underwater Library.
It was all about jobs.

Henry wondered, "Maybe I should be something other than the leader of the Underwater Big Band?"

The next day, Henry told the Underwater Big Band, "I need to try new things. I hope you can get along without me as your leader."

The band was surprised. They all liked Henry and they did not want to stand in his way.

"We wish you the best,"
Jacques the Shark said.

Henry didn't know which job
to try first. He saw Captain
Feathersword's ship.
"That's it!" Henry exclaimed. "I
already love the sea. I'll become
the captain of a pirate ship!"

"I want to find out what it is
like to be a pirate," Henry said.

Captain Feathersword clapped Henry on the back. "Ahoy there, me hearty! It's the greatest job on all the seven seas."

Then he told Henry, "The only way to learn is by experience. Why don't you take the wheel while I have a nap?"

Henry took the wheel. He was all right, as long as the sea was calm. But when the wind started picking up, Henry didn't know what to do!

Suddenly, the wheel spun out of control. Henry became tangled in its spokes. "Captain Feathersword!" Henry shouted.

Captain Feathersword and The Wiggles grabbed Henry. They pulled with all their might.

THWIP! THUMP!
BUMP! SPLASH!

Finally, they freed Henry.
The Wiggles thumped back
onto the deck. Henry went
flying overboard into the sea!

When Henry was back on deck, he decided he didn't want to be a pirate anymore. "There are plenty of jobs for me on land," Henry told himself.

As he was crossing a street,
Henry saw Officer Beaples
directing traffic.
"That looks like fun!"
Henry exclaimed.

Soon, Henry was wearing his
very own police uniform.

But since Henry's eight legs all pointed in different directions, the drivers got confused. Henry had caused a traffic jam!

"It's all my fault," Henry told
   Officer Beaples.
"No one is good at everything,
   Henry," the kind officer replied.

But I must be good at something,
Henry thought. He went back
to the library and made a list of
new jobs.

Henry tried to be an astronaut,
but all the space suits had only
two arms and two legs.

Henry found that he was a very
fast artist. Henry could paint
eight paintings at a time!
Unfortunately, he also made
eight times the mess.

"Hmmm . . ." Henry sighed. "I have too many legs, but there must be something I can do. I miss my friends in the Underwater Big Band."

The Wiggles knew that the
Underwater Big Band needed
Henry as much as he needed them.
"Why don't you go see them?"
Murray suggested.

When they reached the
rehearsal, Jeff tugged at his
ears. "This doesn't sound like
the Underwater Big Band."

The musicians saw Henry
and The Wiggles. They put
down their instruments
and cheered, "Henry!"

Henry picked up eight batons and started conducting with all of them at once.

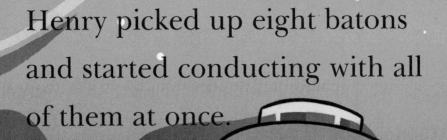

"They're eight times better!"
Murray said.

Soon, all The Wiggles were
wiggling underwater to the
music.

"I'm glad I tried different jobs," Henry said. "Now I really appreciate doing what I do best. Let's play it once more from the top!"